Vera Pratt
and the
False Moustaches

BROUGH GIRLING

Illustrated by Tony Blundell

PUFFIN BOOKS

Puffin Books, Penguin Books Ltd, Harmondsworth, Middlesex, England
Viking Penguin Inc., 40 West 23rd Street, New York, New York 10010, U.S.A.
Penguin Books Australia Ltd, Ringwood, Victoria, Australia
Penguin Books Canada Ltd, 2801 John Street, Markham, Ontario, Canada L3R 1B4
Penguin Books (N.Z.) Ltd, 182–190 Wairau Road, Auckland 10, New Zealand

First published 1987

Phototypeset in Linotron Bembo by
Rowland Phototypesetting Ltd,
Bury St Edmunds, Suffolk
Made and printed in Great Britain by
Cox & Wyman Ltd, Reading, Berks

Puffin Books

VERA PRATT AND
THE FALSE MOUSTACHES

Vera Pratt is no ordinary mum. She spends more time poking about in engines and polishing her motorbike leathers than cooking or cleaning her house, as some mums do. Wally, her son, wishes she was a bit more 'normal' and that living at home wasn't like living in a garage – but one day something happens which makes him gladder than ever to have Vera, the fanatic mechanic, as a mum.

It all started with a game of Frisbee, and a confrontation with Captain Smoothy-Smythe, the local garage owner – but suddenly Wally and his friends are caught up in a real 'cops and robbers' adventure. Except that this time there are no cops to help them – only Vera. Could she foil the Captain's evil plot, and where did this adventure spring from anyway? For the answer to that question (and how false moustaches come into it) you'll have to read on!

Brough Girling is a freelance writer and promotions consultant in the book trade. For the past fifteen years he has worked with Books for Students and since 1984 he has been campaign director of READATHON (their national sponsored reading week). He lives in the Cotswolds and never wears a false moustache, except when visiting his bank manager.

For Sam and Barnaby

Contents

Vera Pratt and Her Son

'Help!' said Mrs Vera Pratt.

She was standing in her kitchen, surrounded by pieces of motorbike.

'What's up, Mum?' said Wally.

'It's this blooming bike!' she said. 'I'll never get the wretched thing together again. The grunion pins are all gunged up and the sprockets have gone on the overhead cams.' She wiped a small tear from her cheek with the corner of an oily rag.

'Perhaps we should just put it all in the dustbin, and buy a car,' said Wally.

'Don't be a wally, Wally,' she replied. 'We don't need a car, after all there's only the two of us, and cars are very difficult to maintain. I mean, how can you get a car into the kitchen to strip the gearbox out? With a bike it's easy.'

Wally could see what she meant, but he still longed for her to change her mind. Sometimes he wished his mother was more like the mothers in the ads on telly.

'Just wait till I've drained this crankcase, then I suppose I'll have to get you some breakfast,' she said.

Wally decided to head for the living-room, where the television was, but he had only moved a pace or two when he heard one of his mother's favourite expressions: 'Knicker elastic!'

'What's up, Mum?' he asked again.

'This motorbike, Wally, will be the death of me!'

'Well, they are very dangerous,' replied Wally, thoughtfully.

'Not on the road, twit-face! In here! I'll never get it together again. Oh dear, where on earth have I put the spigot-nut from this timing-chain case?'

Wally helped her look. Every surface in the kitch-en, including the draining-board, was covered with bits of motorbike and engine, and Wally didn't know what he was looking for.

'Sorry Mum,' he said, 'I can't see a spigot-chain cover for a nut-case anywhere!'

Then the phone rang.

'OhDearOhLor!' said Wally's mum in exasperation. 'Wally, answer that phone while I get these tappets back in their rocker cover . . . I don't know,' she continued, '. . . a woman's work is never done!'

'Hello,' said Wally. 'Wally Pratt here.'

'Hello,' said a voice on the phone.

'Who's there, please?' asked Wally.

'April Fool,' said the voice.

'Hey Mum,' said Wally, putting his hand over the mouthpiece of the phone, 'there's someone on the phone playing us an April fool trick!'

'That's all I blinking well need!' said Mrs Pratt. 'Just give me that phone! I'll teach them to play April fool jokes on us in the middle of August!'

And she took the phone, rather roughly for a mother, from Wally.

'Now look here!' she said into it. 'I've got quite enough to do with my fat little son to feed and a Honda XL 580 with electric starter to put back together without a silly April fool phoney phone calls to deal with! Thank you very much!'

'But Aunt Vera!' said the voice.

'What!' said Wally's mother.

'Aunt Vera, it's April, your niece, April Phoole.'

'OH!' said Mrs Pratt. 'Oh now I see! Well now, April, how are you? How lovely to hear from you!'

Mrs Pratt had temporarily forgotten that she had a niece called April Phoole.

'I'm fine thank you, Aunt Vera. I was wondering if I could come and stay with you and Wally. I'm on holiday and I fancy a change of scenery. Could I come tomorrow? There's a train which gets in at half-past twelve.'

'Yes!' said Mrs Pratt, who always made up her mind quickly about things. 'We'll meet you.'

'Can I bring my dog?' asked April.

'Yes!' said Wally's mother firmly.

'Thank you, and as I'm hoping to be on Bags of Fun this week, could you take me to the television studios in London?'

'What on earth is Bags of Fun?' asked her aunt.

'It's a TV quiz programme, Wally will tell you all about it.'

'OK,' said Mrs Pratt. 'Bye!'

'Bye.'

Vera Pratt put the phone down.

'Knicker elastic!' she shouted. 'That's put us in a fine old pickle!' And she scowled, picked up a monkey-wrench and turned her attention to her pieces of motorbike.

'Why has that put us in a pickle, Mum?' said Wally.

'Because, Wally, if we meet her off the train tomorrow, let alone take her to London, we've got to get to the station, and even if I get this motorbike back on the road by then, how are you and I and she all going to fit on it?'

'You could go there without me,' said Wally brightly.

'Don't be daft, Wally, she's bringing her dog!' snapped his mother.

'So?'

'Think, lad!' said Mrs Pratt, 'We haven't got a crash helmet for a dog!!!'

'What are we going to do then, Mum?' asked Wally.

'I'll think of something!' she replied. 'Now why don't you get out of my kitchen – I can't reassemble a 500 cc engine with you under my feet all the time, now can I?' She wiped her oily hands on the front of her pinny as she said it.

Then the door-bell rang, and Wally went to see who it was.

On the door-step stood three boys.

The first was called Bean Pole. He may have had another, more sensible name, but he was always known as Bean Pole, probably because he was lanky and thin.

Bean Pole and Wally Pratt were great friends, maybe because they were very different. Wally was a large, round child, and about as nimble as a beached whale. Bean Pole was active. He was always saying, 'Let's do this' or 'Let's do that'.

Behind Bean Pole was a lad called Bill Stickers. His actual name was Bill Stukley, but when friends of his had seen a notice saying BILL STICKERS WILL BE PROSECUTED they had nicknamed him Bill Stickers. He always looked what his mother called 'a mess'. His shirt never stayed tucked in and his hair never stayed 'done'. He looked like a plastic model that had been put together very badly.

The last boy in the group was the youngest, and smallest: his name was Ginger Tom – not because he looked like a cat, but because his first name was Tom and he had red hair and freckles.

'Are you coming out to play, Wally?' asked Bean Pole.

'You bet!' said Wally. 'My mum's in a bit of a bate in the kitchen again.'

'Is that Bean Pole and your friends?' called Wally's mother from the kitchen.

'Yes Mum. We're going out!'

'Tell you what,' said his mother, coming to the door, 'yesterday when I was out shopping I went to the ABC Garage to get some heavy-duty hypoid gear and axle grease, and I also bought a can of oil

and they gave me this Frisbee thing free with it.
Take it with you!'

'Let's!' said Bean Pole.

And off they all went.

2

The Car Dealers

The ABC Garage looked more or less like any small-town garage. It was set back from the road, and had petrol pumps in front of it and a row of cars that were for sale at the side. Between the pumps and the road itself there was a patch of grubby grass which was surrounded by a few large stones that someone had painted white.

Inside this garage, if you had ever cared to visit it, you would have found at least two car dealers.

Captain Smoothy-Smythe was one of them. He looked like a retired military man. He seemed very upright and smart. He wore a well-cut dark blue blazer with bright brass buttons, check trousers and brown suede shoes.

A pale blue handkerchief stuck out of his breast pocket and he had a moustache that looked carefully groomed.

However, the Captain was a deceiver. For a start he was not really a captain at all. He may have been captain in a football team, long ago, at school, but he had never even been in the army or the navy!

Captain Smoothy-Smythe had an assistant who, unlike his lord and master, was *exactly* what he appeared to be.

He looked like a creepy little rat, and that is what he was. The man's name was Dud Cheque.

His first name was actually Dudley. His mother had given him this name for a special reason. Long before he was born she had been to Dudley Zoo, near Birmingham.

She had always remembered the armadillos in the zoo, with their shuffling round-shouldered way of walking, and their dark mean eyes and long snouts.

When, later in her life, she had had a son who had the same round-shouldered look, dark mean eyes and long snout, it had seemed natural to call him Dudley. Well, you can't really call a child Armadillo Cheque, can you?

The ABC Garage was owned and run by Captain Smoothy-Smythe, who had recently bought it and at the same time had taken on Dud Cheque to do some car-selling and general running around – things like manning the petrol pumps and adding the paraffin to the petrol to make it go a bit further.

The police called at the garage quite regularly, usually looking for cars that had been stolen, and when this happened Dud had to take all the second-hand cars from the forecourt to a nearby railway yard while the Captain kept the officers talking.

At about the same time as Wally Pratt and his friends were going out to play with the new Frisbee the Captain was standing outside his beloved garage, beside a ladder.

Up at the top of the ladder stood Dud Cheque, and under his arm he had a large plastic letter D.

'Cheque! You blundering dunderhead!' said the Captain to his assistant.

'Yes, Guv?' said Dud Cheque.

'Just put the blasted thing up and stop messing about, man!'

'I'm trying to, Guv, but I'm scared I might slip and fall off.'

'Don't be so dim, half-wit! Anyway if you did fall orf you'd probably only land on your thick head, so you wouldn't do yourself any harm. It might do you some good!' And the Captain chuckled to himself at his little joke.

After a lot more shouting by the Captain, and a lot of ladder-wobbling by Dud Cheque, the large letter D was finally fixed on the front wall of the garage at the end of A, B and C.

When Dud, who obviously did not like heights, finally returned to earth, the name along the front of the building said 'ABCD GARAGE'.

'How daft!' he grumbled under his breath as he took the ladder round to the back of the garage. 'Whoever heard of something called the ABCD something-or-other? What's wrong with ABC? It don't make no sense!'

However, to Captain Smoothy-Smythe it made a lot of sense.

Although he was, as you know, sole proprietor and proud owner of the ABC Garage, he knew something that all cheats and villains know. He knew that you can only make extra money from extra activity.

No successful small-time crook gets anywhere if he specializes too deeply in one activity. You have to keep your wits about you and keep an eye open for new opportunities.

When the Captain bought the garage he had quite quickly spotted an opening – a chance to make some extra money.

Most people with important jobs have associations to which they belong. Doctors belong to the British Medical Association; dentists join the British Dental Association. Teachers join the National Union of Teachers and even parents join the PTA – the Parent Teacher Association.

The Captain, in his crafty way, had realized that there was no organization for people like him. What he needed was an organization where people could exchange views and racing tips, and discuss professional things like the latest ways of getting round the VAT man and avoiding income tax – where there could be a frank and open exchange of information about cars.

If you had a dark blue Cortina without a log-

book or registration document, and someone else
had a log-book or registration document for a dark
blue Cortina, and no Cortina, you could come to
some agreement to unite the two.

Spotting that there was no professional body to
represent his needs, Captain Smoothy-Smythe had
done an intelligent and enterprising thing. He had
invented one, and he, being its founder, had nomi-
nated and elected himself President and Treasurer.

His association was called – and this is why he had
added the D to the ABC Garage – the Association of
Bent Car Dealers!

3

The ABCD Garage

Now the Association of Bent Car Dealers was not
an association for people who sold bent cars. It was
simply for people who went about the business of
selling cars in a dishonest way. It was the dealers
who were 'bent', not the cars, although of course as
it happens many members did – quite often – sell
cars that were bent, though with the naked eye and
no experience you might not instantly detect it.

The Captain had realized that an Association of
Bent Car Dealers would have to be a *secret* organization. He had had quite enough trouble from the
police and the income tax man to know that if you
are a Bent Car Dealer the best thing is to keep quiet
about it.

So the ABCD was, from the outset, an under-
cover organization. However, as I have said, the
Captain had only founded the Association in order
to make money. He did this by getting as many
people as possible to join, and then keeping all their
membership money. It was also vital that while
members of the Association needed to keep quiet

where the tax men or police were concerned, they did need to be able to recognize each other – otherwise they would never be able to indulge in the frank exchange of views, betting tips, fake five-pound notes and stolen log-books.

This is what the cunning Captain devised:

Members of the Association would wear a special uniform to show each other that they were members. This consisted of special sheepskin coats like the ones that football commentators on television wear, thin black false moustaches, and large rings that looked like small gold coins held in place by a claw. You don't need me to tell you that the ones the Captain gave out were not made of real gold.

Members who had paid their joining fees received not only all these items free but also an Association Rule Book and a horrible purple Association tie.

Captain Smoothy-Smythe also kept the fact that the ABCD Garage was the Association's headquarters absolutely secret. Members might recognize the initials of the Association in the garage's name, but he certainly didn't want little crooks like Dud Cheque finding out about it. That could lead to too many people getting to hear about the Association, which could mean the police coming round.

The last thing in the world he wanted was the police getting their hands on either the Association's cash or its precious list of members.

If the list fell into their hands he would be drummed out of the motor trade in absolute disgrace: he'd have to struggle to find anywhere to buy another gallon of petrol!

For this reason the Captain actually ran the Association from the back of his car, a rather magnificent vintage Jaguar, which he was always boasting about because he had bought it for only a hundred pounds from a widow who knew nothing at all about cars.

He had had the back seat adapted by his mechanics so that you could tip it up, and underneath it there was a large cavity in which he concealed supplies of the Association's uniforms and Rule Books.

In the boot of the car he had bolted a safe where the Association's precious records and money were hidden.

When Smoothy-Smythe had some spare time on his hands he simply got into the Jaguar and made a short tour of some new neighbourhood. He'd call in at garages, back-street welding shops and scrap-yards, and recruit a few more members to the cause!

You will understand from this that the Captain had several reasons for being very proud of his old red Jaguar and was rather pleased with his Associa-tion of Bent Car Dealers. As a scheme to bring in more money it had everything one could ask for: it was neat, smooth and efficient, and the police didn't know about it!

There was only one thing wrong with the ABCD Garage in the Captain's opinion: his assistant. He suspected that Dud Cheque was stupid and lazy. The Captain decided to try to improve things, and he thought that the best way to encourage Dud to do his best was to scare him!

'Come into my office, Cheque, would you, old boy,' he said to Dud, who had put the ladder back behind the garage and was now grinding the chassis number off a Ford Granada.

'OK Guv,' said Dud, out of the side of his mouth.

Within moments, Dud Cheque and his military-looking employer were sitting on either side of the Captain's large second-hand desk. His office was at the front of the garage, with a good view over the road and the petrol pumps.

'Now look here, Cheque, old man,' said the Captain firmly, 'you and I have been together in this garage for almost three weeks and I can't see that so far I, or my jolly old business, have benefited one iota from the arrangement.'

'What's a iota?' said Dud, who thought it sounded like an Italian car.

'An iota, squire,' said the Captain, 'is a small, tiny particle – a little piece of something – something about the size, now I come to think of it, of your brain-box!

'What I am saying, iota-bonce, is that you are under-performing. You are about as much use as a race-horse with three legs. You skulk around the workshop like a rat with a hangover and you're doing me no good – no good at all!'

'Oh?' said Dud. 'Well, I cleans the cars, don't I?'

'It's not CLEANING cars that makes money, half-wit,' said the Captain. 'It's SELLING them!'

'I gets 'em ready to sell,' replied Dud Cheque. 'And who washes 'em? – who puts the sawdust into the engines to make them sound quieter? – who wires up the exhausts so they don't fall off on road tests? – who stops up the radiators with chewing-gum so they don't leak? I does!'

'I'M NOT TALKING ABOUT PRE-DELIVERY INSPECTIONS, CHEQUE!' re-

torted the Captain loudly. 'I'm talking about
actually generating the sales, making some jolly old
cash! If you don't do something profitable pretty
soon you'll be out on your ear! Get it?'

'Yes Guv,' said Dud Cheque humbly.

'Impress me, Cheque,' snarled the Captain. 'Impress me with a deal, a scheme, a wheeze – before
the end of this week, or it's the sack for you, buddy
boy, jolly old curtains!'

Dud slunk back to the workshop.

Now, Dud Cheque didn't do all the work in the

garage – like putting the sawdust into the engines, gumming up the radiators, grinding off the chassis numbers – on his own.

He was handy at all these simple tasks, but he was no great mechanic. If the Captain needed to take the engine out of a car rather quickly, or needed for instance to weld the front end of one car on to the back end of another one, or to change the colour of one a bit smartish before the police came round again, he used mechanics. He had on his staff two brothers, Grimey and Slimey O'Reilly.

Grimey and Slimey O'Reilly spent most of their lives underneath cars. They wore overalls which were the colour of used engine oil. Their fingernails were as black as coal!

Grimey and Slimey O'Reilly were idling the time away making up a few false number-plates when Dud Cheque returned from the Captain's office.

'The Guv says I've got to impress him,' said Dud dejectedly.

'And how are you going to do that?' asked Grimey O'Reilly, who instantly saw that Dud had a big problem.

'Dunno,' said Dud, sitting down on a drum of recently syphoned petrol and lighting a cigarette.

4

The Flight of the Frisbee

The boys had taken the new Frisbee to an area called Old Codger's Wood, which was beside the ABCD Garage. It was not a very good place for Frisbee-throwing. It was not open enough, having too many bushes and trees in it. However, they messed around for a while. They half-built a den, dammed a stream and let the water go again, and climbed several trees. Bill Stickers, who looked rather untidy before he got there, ruined a fairly new pair of shoes and tore his anorak.

'Let's go back to the recreation ground!' said Bean Pole eventually. 'We can throw the new Frisbee there.'

'OK,' said Wally, who had had quite enough exercise for one morning.

The recreation ground was a large open field just opposite Wally Pratt's house. It had a football pitch and a small cricket pavilion as well as swings and slides. In one corner, near the road, there was a large shallow duck-pond.

As they came out of the corner of the wood the

bright morning air seemed to work a refreshing
magic on the frame of Wally Pratt.

'Hey Bean Pole!' he said suddenly. 'I fancy giving
that Frisbee a chuck right now!'

'What, in the road?'

'Yeah,' said Wally, 'I can control it. I could land it
on any spot you like to name. Betcha!'

'Oh yeah, cocky-boots!' said Bill Stickers. 'How
come you think you are so good with a Frisbee?'

'I can do it! I'm quite handy at throwing things,'
said Wally Pratt.

In many ways he was quite right. Although
Wally was, as I have said, a large boy and rather a
lazy one, he was very strong and his ability to put in
short sharp bursts of action was quite impressive.

For instance, if he didn't like something someone
in the school playground said, he could get them
down and sit on them before they could say Jack
Robinson or 'Sorry Wally'.

'OK,' said Bean Pole. 'Land it on that piece of grass in front of the ABC Garage, where those white painted stones are.'

'Bet you can't!' said Ginger Tom, egging him on.

They were still some distance from the garage, but Wally didn't want to admit that he thought the target was a little too far away.

'OK,' he said.

When you want to throw a Frisbee a long way, accuracy is sometimes sacrificed.

Wally brought his right arm back, backhand style, in front of his body. He gave the disc a hefty jerk, and he did what all successful Frisbee-throwers do – he concentrated on the final flick of the wrist. It is this that gives a Frisbee its special, helicopter-like characteristics. If you don't get that flick and the spin right, you might as well be dropping dinner plates out of an upstairs window.

The Frisbee left Wally's hand and started on its

flight towards the piece of grass at the front of the garage. It left him at about waist height, and flew straight and true.

'Told you!' said Wally Pratt, with triumph in his voice. The boys were impressed.

But Wally had spoken too soon.

The Frisbee veered away from the road and went straight towards the side of the garage.

The boys held their breath as it headed directly for the row of cars that were parked there, ready for sale.

They could hardly believe what happened next.

The Frisbee went straight through the open sun-roof of one of the cars, and landed almost noiselessly inside it, probably on the driver's seat.

To be even more precise, it went straight through the open sunroof of a magnificent red vintage Jaguar.

It was the Captain's Jaguar, of which only you, and I, and Captain Smoothy-Smythe himself, know the secrets. He had returned early that morning from a particularly successful recruiting drive. The safe in the boot was extremely full of money!

'Blimmin'eck!' said Wally. 'Can you believe it, Bean Pole?'

'What?'

'That it went through the open roof of that old car,' said Wally.

'No,' said Bean Pole. 'But I think it did!'

'I think it did too,' said Bill Stickers.

'So do I,' said Ginger Tom. 'All we've got to do is get it back.'

'That's right,' said Wally, looking worried.

They advanced on the garage carefully, not sure that their luck would hold.

It didn't.

Captain Smoothy-Smythe had been pleased with the success of his recent recruitment drive for the Association of Bent Car Dealers. He had purposely left the car at the side of the garage so that it was close to the door of his office. He needed to fill up the space under the back seat with some items of the Association's uniform.

The sheepskin coats were bulky, so he usually topped up the car with supplies of them after dark, when he could be sure that creeps like Dud Cheque and the O'Reilly brothers wouldn't spot him. But on this last trip he had used up rather a lot of false moustaches.

The demand for false moustaches was very unpredictable: sometimes the Captain would have a recruiting campaign and most of the new members he enrolled in the Association would have very nice, thin black moustaches of their own, just as the Association's Rule Book demanded. There was then no need to give them false ones.

This last trip, however, had very nearly emptied his last box of 'Mr Spiv's Special Stick-On Mous-

taches'. He had another box of them in the safe in his office and he intended to pop them into the compartment under the back seat of the car while he remembered.

He was returning to the car with the box of Mr Spiv's Special Stick-Ons when he thought he heard the noise of something hitting the inside of the precious Jaguar.

Have you ever noticed how, if you are feeling guilty about something and trying to keep secret about it, anything to do with it makes you feel jumpy?

The Captain jumped when he thought he heard something hit the Jag.

He shot back into his office and stuffed the guilty box of Special Stick-Ons back into the safe. He then raced outside again ready to be charming in case it was the police.

At the door of the garage he took a good look round, like a sentry who has just heard a twig break.

Approaching the Jaguar – headquarters of the Association of Bent Car Dealers, of which the Captain was President and Treasurer for life – were four scruffy boys.

'Bean Pole?' whispered Wally when they were nearly up to the car.

'Yer,' whispered back Bean Pole.

'The windows are closed, and if I open the door someone will hear.'

'So?' said Bean Pole.

'So you'll have to reach in through the roof,' explained Wally.

'We'll all give you a leg up.'

'OK,' said Bean Pole, reluctantly.

The boys got to the car and looked into it. The Frisbee was visible, lodged upright between the two front seats.

Wally, Bill and Ginger bent down beside the driver's door, and between them they got hold of Bean Pole's legs and feet.

Just as they lifted, and as Bean Pole reached down with his long arms through the roof of the car, 'OI!' shouted the Captain, 'BUZZ ORF!'

5

Bean Pole Attempts a Rescue

I don't know how you would react if a military-looking man, rather red in the face and with a thin moustache, were to shout 'OI . . . BUZZ ORF!' at you.

But I do know how Wally Pratt, Bean Pole, Bill Stickers and Ginger Tom reacted. They ran.

They ran towards home – it always seems the safest direction to take in this sort of situation, and they were spurred on as they went by additional shouts from the Captain of 'Little blighters!', 'Clear off!' and 'If I catch you . . .'

Luckily they could quickly tell that the Captain wasn't going to catch them, because he was not actually giving chase.

'You know what?' said Wally when they were safely out of sight of the garage.

'What?' said the others, getting their breath back.

'We've gone and lost my mum's Frisbee! The first thing she'll want to know when I get home is what I've done with it.'

The four of them were walking now, panting.

They were going up a hill that led on to the recreation field and Wally's house.

Just as they were all thinking of Wally's mother, she came into view. She was roaring down the hill towards them, on her motorbike.

'Would you believe it!' said Wally. 'She's got the bike going again!'

'She's a miracle, your mother,' said Ginger. 'How does she do it?'

'Search me,' said Wally. 'She sometimes gets very determined.'

With a roar of throaty engine Mrs Vera Pratt swept past them. She didn't slow down, but she

gave a small wave as she shot past in red racing leathers, crash helmet and oily pinny. Wally thought he could see a satisfied gleam in her eye, behind the goggles.

The boys walked on towards home in thoughtful silence. It was broken eventually by Bean Pole.

'You know, Wally,' he said, 'I think we went about getting that Frisbee back in the wrong way. Our tactics were all wrong.'

'Well, how should we have done it?' replied Wally. 'Because I tell you what, if there is a better way I think we ought to try it. I don't fancy having to tell my mum I've lost it.'

'I don't blame you!' said Bill Stickers.

'Well,' explained Bean Pole, 'that posh geezer down at the garage only got cross because he thought we were going to harm his beautiful old car. He thought we were messing about near it. We should have been braver and a bit cleverer. After all, we'd done no harm. We should have gone and seen him first, told him what had happened, and asked him politely for our Frisbee back.'

'Oh yeah?' said Ginger Tom. 'Well, we can't do that now: he'd string us up!'

'That's right!' added Bill. 'He'd skin us alive.'

'He might not if we flattered him a bit,' said Bean Pole. 'If we told him how beautiful the car is and things like that. Anyway, what's the alternative? I don't mind having a go at it!'

'You're joking!' said Wally, wondering if Bean Pole had gone soft in the head.

'No I'm not,' replied Bean Pole. 'It's worth a try. If he gets nasty we can always run. He won't catch us.'

'Well, I suppose it's worth a go,' said Wally to the others. He was secretly impressed by Bean Pole's bravery, but felt nervous.

'Come on then,' said Bean Pole enthusiastically.

And they all turned round and started to walk back towards the ABCD Garage.

When they got there they couldn't see the Jaguar.

'I bet he's taken it round the back,' said Wally. 'And that'll mean that he's seen the Frisbee, and he'll either have put it in the bin, or taken it inside.'

'Come on,' said Bean Pole, 'it's still worth a try.'

They got to the petrol pumps and – without any further discussion of the dangers of the actions they were about to take – Bean Pole led them straight towards Captain Smoothy-Smythe's office door.

I should now tell you what had happened after the Captain had yelled 'Oi! Buzz orf!' and 'Little blighters!'

As you can imagine, he was extremely relieved that it had only been boys near the Jaguar and not the police. He had shouted at them, and then had gone back to his office.

However, he had completely forgotten the fact

that the Jag's secret compartment was dangerously low on Mr Spiv's Special Stick-On Moustaches, and he had begun to get on with all the bits and bobs that running a successful business like his entails.

He had put some large bills into the waste-paper basket, and he had written a couple of threatening letters. Then he had had a quick look through the *Sporting Life*, the horse-racing newspaper. Then he had gone on an official tour of inspection round the workshop.

He had a word with his two loyal servants, Slimey and Grimey O'Reilly, who were both idling away the time winding back the speedo on an extremely rusty Lancia that the Captain was hoping to sell rather quickly.

'Ah,' he said. 'How's it going, lads?'

'All right, Guv,' said Grimey. 'We're just now carrying out the pre-delivery inspection on this one.'

'That's it, men,' said the Captain, to encourage them. 'I want it in showroom condition!'

'Oh yes, Surr,' said Slimey. 'It's only done thirty thousand miles, Surr.'

'Twenty-one thousand now,' said Grimey, correcting him from beneath the dashboard of the car.

'Jolly good work,' their employer congratulated them, adding, 'Have you seen Dud Cheque around?'

'Well, he was here,' said Slimey, 'but he went out the front. I think he may have popped out.'

'Right-O,' said the Captain. He didn't actually want to see Dud Cheque, but he wanted to check up on his whereabouts. The creepy little rat was beginning to get him down!

As the Captain arrived back at his desk after this tour of the workshops the four boys had arrived by the petrol pumps, and a moment later Bean Pole, lanky and eager as ever, was knocking politely on the open door of the Captain's office.

The Captain looked up. Bean Pole, Wally, Bill and Ginger looked down. The Captain opened

his mouth but, before he could speak, Bean Pole spoke.

'We're very sorry, Sir,' he said. 'We weren't doing any harm.'

This slightly took the wind out of the Captain's sails. 'But I saw you, you little blighters. You were putting your sticky little fingers all over my best motor-car,' he said – but he wasn't shouting.

Bean Pole, encouraged by the lack of volume in the Captain's voice, postponed any plans to run for it, and Wally, Bill and Ginger behind him tried unsuccessfully to blend in with the furniture.

'Yes Sir, we're sorry Sir, but we were just admiring the car Sir,' said Bean Pole.

'I see,' said the Captain. For obvious reasons he didn't much like people admiring the car; but he could agree that it was worth admiring.

'It's a Jaguar, isn't it Sir?' chipped in Bill Stickers, who was beginning to get the hang of Bean Pole's new tactics.

'Yes,' said the Captain. 'Rather a rare one, actually.'

'It's a really beautiful car,' added Wally Pratt.

'Yes,' said the Captain.

The boys realized that although this meeting with the Captain was quite chummy and no one was shouting or running, it wasn't really getting to the point. It didn't seem to be getting the Frisbee back. The Captain's next sentence helped.

'Well,' he said, 'I don't suppose you've come here just to say you're sorry. Are you after something? Car stickers or posters or something?'

He would gladly have given them anything just to get them off the premises. The Captain didn't like visitors at the garage.

'Well, that's the point,' said Bean Pole. 'You see, we were admiring the car because, just by accident, our new Frisbee had just kind of dropped in through the sunroof.'

Wally, Bill and Ginger held their breath and checked on the exact position of the office door.

'So you've come back for this Frisbee thing, have you?' asked the Captain rather sternly.

'Yes Sir,' said Bean Pole, looking as downcast and guilty as he possibly could.

'Oh, very well,' said the Captain impatiently, 'let's go and get it. And,' he added, firmly, 'let this be a lesson to you!'

'Yes Sir,' said the boys, not sure what 'let this be a lesson to you' meant, but sensing that they were going to get their Frisbee back. Bean Pole's tactics seemed to be working!

The Captain stood up and walked towards the door. The boys parted to let him through, and then followed him.

They followed him past the pumps and out on to the forecourt, not far from the grass where the Frisbee should have landed. They followed him from there to the area where the cars for sale stood, and where the red Jaguar had been.

The Captain stopped.

'My Gawd,' he said. 'WHERE THE HELL'S MY MOTOR!'

He went rather red in the face; and deep inside his dark blue blazer his heart started pounding like a piston.

'SOMEONE'S MOVED MY MOTOR!'

The boys, as we know, had already noticed this, but they had the good sense not to point it out.

Although a spare set of keys to the Jaguar was kept on a board in the workshop, the Captain did not allow anyone to move the car, because he didn't want people poking about inside it.

'SOMEONE'S NICKED MY MOTOR!' shouted the Captain, panic creeping into his voice. He shouted it towards the open doors at the side of the workshop.

Slimey and Grimey appeared, but their gormless expressions showed that they knew nothing about it.

Dud realized that he had made some kind of mistake.

He could see, for instance, that Captain Smoothy-Smythe turned purple and jumped up and down, and had already hurt himself by kicking a large white painted stone.

I will try to translate into respectable English some of the things he was shouting.

'CHEQUE, YOU RAT-FINK OAF! PIN-HEAD! DUMBO! BELLYBUM IDIOT! I'd like

to use your head as a road block! I've a good mind to turn you inside-out! NUMSKULL!'

Dud was now certain that he had done something wrong.

'Hang on, Guv,' he said. 'You told me to be impressive . . .'

'Impressive!' interrupted his boss, shouting, 'I'd like to impress you in two metres of wet cement!'

'But you only paid a hundred quid for that old car – and I've got you a thousand *and* a motorbike!' protested Dud, still not sure what he had done wrong.

'A THOUSAND!' roared the Captain. 'A MEASLY THOUSAND! That car was worth TEN thousand, and a lot more besides!'

Dud opened and closed his mouth a few times, but didn't say anything.

'There's only one way, Cheque, that you can save your miserable repulsive little skin. Get that car back! Get it back now, pronto, or else. JOLLY OLD ELSE!'

And the Captain stormed off, back into his office, his head whirling with images of sheepskin coats, false rings and moustaches, a safe full to the brim with newly collected money and lists of Bent Car Dealers' names and addresses, and visits from the police!

Wally Pratt, Bean Pole, Bill Stickers and Ginger Tom could see quite clearly that Wally's mother had now solved the problem of the lost Frisbee. It looked as if she had bought it along with a very impressive motor-car.

They retreated from the scene, and started the long walk home.

The Captain walked to his office and sat down behind his desk. He surveyed in his mind the ruins of his empire.

He poured himself two large gins from his gin bottle. The seriousness of the situation filled his thoughts. He had lost a magnificent car for a sum that was a fraction of its real value, and the Association of Bent Car Dealers, which had promised to bring him so much joy and profit, was smashed to smithereens.

Then he wondered if he had been right in trying to terrorize Dud Cheque into getting the car back without delay. He knew that this was his only hope – he had to get the Jaguar back before Mrs Pratt explored its depths too deeply – before she got her hands on the cash in the boot or became suspicious about the gear under the back seat and called in the police. But what chance would Dud Cheque have of getting it back?

Captain Smoothy-Smythe drained his glass, and stared into space as he thought about it all. He realized, as his colour slowly returned to normal, that the situation required tactics.

You will remember that when Wally and the boys first wanted to get their Frisbee back they had simply tried to grab it. Their direct approach to a crisis had not worked, and they had learnt from this experience to try some tact, flattery and guile. Only fools rush in: wise men tread more carefully.

The Captain, older and wiser than the boys, already knew this simple truth. The more he thought about it the more he realized that it had been bad tactics simply to yell at Dud Cheque and urge him to get the car back, pronto. After all, Dud Cheque was a snivelling oaf who would probably mess the whole thing up even more.

What was needed was charm, flattery and straightforward deceit. He, the Captain, would go and see this Pratt woman himself. He had a way with women, and would soon persuade the empty-headed creature to return the car and have her money and motorbike back.

He went into the workshop. 'Cheque!' he called. 'Come into my office!'

Dud Cheque got up dejectedly from a pile of re-cut tyres that he had been sitting on, and shuffled into his tyrant's office.

'Look here, Cheque,' said the Captain, mopping his brow with the handkerchief from the breast pocket of his blazer, 'I may have been a bit too hasty with you just now. Sit down.'

Dud sat down.

'You have made a monumental mess-up, old boy,' said the Captain. 'And we are going to have to put it right. We are going to have to indulge in what we used to call in the army "damage limitation".' (I don't have to remind you that the Captain had never been in the army.) 'I quite see that you'll need my help in getting the old girl to part with the car again and have her bike back, so we'll go and see her together and I'll talk her round. You just leave it all to me.'

And so, moments later, Dud Cheque and his boss started off up the hill towards Mrs Pratt's house. 'This is going to be a push-over,' said the Captain to himself, 'a Jolly Old Push-Over!'

Wally and his three friends had already arrived home, and as it was getting dark they were upstairs reading comics.

7

The Captain Attempts a Rescue

A few moments later there was a knock on Vera Pratt's front door.

'Wally!' she called from the kitchen, 'there's someone at the door, answer it, will you.'

'OK Mum!' replied Wally from upstairs, where he and Bean Pole and Ginger were by now ankle deep in *Beanos*.

Half-way down the stairs Wally glanced through a small window which looked out on to the front garden. What he saw made him shudder.

There on the step stood Captain Smoothy-Smythe, proprietor of the ABCD Garage, and his horrible little assistant, Dudley Cheque.

'Could you go, Mum?' shouted Wally. 'I think I've suddenly got to go to the lavatory!' And he rushed back upstairs to the boys.

'It's that fierce bloke from the garage!' he whispered earnestly to them. 'I bet he's changed his mind and has come to moan about us to my mum. She'll slaughter me!'

'Let's get out of here quick!' said Bean Pole, but

they all knew that it was hopeless. There was no way out of the house other than through the front hall. They were trapped: all they could do was go to the top of the stairs and listen to the trouble brewing below them.

'Blooming boy!' said Mrs Pratt under her breath as she wiped her oily hands on her pinny and walked

to the front door. 'It's all he's any good for – going to the lavatory.'

And she opened the front door.

'Ah, Mrs Pratt, I presume,' said the Captain, smiling at her.

'So what if it is!' she replied, with her hands on her hips.

'Ah . . . well,' said the Captain.

'I said, "So what if it is",' said Mrs Pratt again.

'Well, Madam,' said the Captain. 'As you know, you purchased this old car from my assistant here, this afternoon.' And he pointed first to the Jaguar which was standing by the front gate, and then to the shamefaced Dud Cheque.

'Yes,' said Mrs Pratt, 'I know that, thank you very much.'

'Well,' said the Captain, realizing that he was having difficulty getting into his stride with the conversation, 'I'm afraid there is a bit of a problem.'

'Oh?' replied Wally's mother in a haughty voice. She had taken an instant dislike to the Captain.

'Yes, my little friend here made a bit of a mistake: the car, you see, was not really for sale.'

'Well, he sold it to me!' said the new owner. The boys upstairs sat fascinated. What on earth was going to happen next?

'Ah . . . but you see it is really far too old to be put to everyday use, and I'm sure that a woman as attractive and charming and modern as you,' oiled the Captain, 'would be far better off with some-thing more up-to-date. Now I happen to have a very nice Lancia that's only done thirty . . . er . . . I mean twenty-one thousand miles. If you would like to return this old wreck I will be delighted to refund your thousand pounds and let you have your motorbike back *and* let you have the Lancia at the very special price of only eight hundred pounds – so you will have saved yourself two hundred pounds, and will have a much more suitable car! Aren't you lucky, my dear.'

He finished his little speech with his best and broadest smile. Then he paused to draw breath, partly because he was out of it, and partly while he wondered what his next move should be.

He reckoned that in normal circumstances the flattery he'd used would have done the trick, but somehow he didn't seem to be getting though to Mrs Pratt.

There was something in the way that she crossed her arms, clenched her large fists and started to sneer at him through her gritted teeth that made him think she might be a tough nut to crack.

'Do I make myself clear, Madam?' he asked.

'Yes, you make yourself clear,' replied Mrs Pratt. 'You must think I'm blooming barmy!'

'Pardon?' said the Captain.

'Yer what?' said Dud Cheque.

'Look, sunshine,' she went on, 'this car is exactly

what I want. I'm fed up with motorbikes, and my
niece is coming to stay tomorrow, and even with a
side-car I can't go traipsing here there and everywhere with my Wally and her and his little friends.
Besides, you can't get crash helmets for dogs – so a
bike's no good to us. I want a nice big strong car,
that can stand up to a bit of my vigorous driving,
and high standards of maintenance! And now that's
what I've got! So why don't you push off back to
your crummy little garage.' And she glared at him,
and started to close the door.

The Captain knew that he was up against a
stubborn lady.

'Look here,' he said firmly. 'This old banger's clapped out. It's as old as the hills. It's had it. It's ancient. Gawd . . .' he added unwisely, 'it goes back to nineteen forty-three!'

'Look, mate!' said Mrs Pratt, straightening her back and putting her hands on her hips again, 'as it happens, I also go back to nineteen forty-three – and I am most certainly not as old as the hills and clapped out, nor have I had it!'

'Oh, for heaven's sake!' said the Captain angrily, and he opened his large wallet and drew out a thick wad of fifty-pound notes. 'Why don't you use a bit of sense, jolly old sense?' He shook the notes at her.

'And,' replied Mrs Pratt firmly, 'why don't you jolly old buzz off!' She wiped her hands on her oily apron again, as if to make sure they were fairly clean before she throttled him.

The Captain and Dud Cheque knew that their tactics had not worked. They did the only thing they could do in the circumstances: they buzzed off.

'Stupid old faggot!' said the Captain as they strode back to the garage.

'What have I done now?' said Dud.

'Not you, dumbo! Her!'

He didn't say anything else for some time, but he thought a lot. She's on to something, he thought. She's found the secret compartment, or she knows the *real* value of the car. Perhaps she's found the loot in the boot!

Captain Smoothy-Smythe brooded long, deep, and darkly on these grim possibilities. He would not be defeated.

8

The Second Day

The next day, the second since this story started, dawned bright and clear.

'Just the sort of day for a really good burn-up in my new old Jag!' said Mrs Vera Pratt to herself as she tucked strands of loose hair into her black leather flying helmet.

'Just the sort of day for not doing too much,' said W. Pratt to himself as he poured out a second heap of cornflakes.

'Just the sort of day for messing about, throwing Frisbees, playing football and having adventures,' said Bean Pole to himself as he swiped the top off his egg.

'Now don't you go ruining any more clothes!' said Bill Stickers's mother.

Ginger Tom was up, breakfasted and out before anyone in his house noticed him.

'Today,' said Captain Smoothy-Smythe to himself as he buttoned up his dark blue blazer, 'today I've got to make plans to get that blasted car back. Jolly, Blasted Got To!'

'I might have a go at impressing the boss again today,' said Dud Cheque to himself as he wiped his nose on his shirt sleeve, before putting his jacket on.

The very first thing that Captain Smoothy-Smythe decided to do when hc got to the ABCD Garage was to summon Dud Cheque once more into his office.

Dud had got to work before the Captain, and was helping the O'Reilly brothers to swap the good new tyres on a Mini Clubman that a little old man had brought in for a service with some old ones that had been stored round the back near the oil tank. They had nearly finished, and were just checking to see if the spare wheel could be given similar treatment, when they heard their master's voice.

'Cheque! Thickhead! Where are you? Come into my office!'

Dud Cheque shuffled, round-shouldered but obedient, towards the office door.

Usually when the Captain called for him in this way it scared Dud Cheque. Was he going to be told off again? Was the Captain going to hit him – with a gin bottle over the head, perhaps? Or was he going to get the sack?

Strange though it may seem, today Dud felt more confident.

After the disasters of the day before he knew that he was in grave danger of parting company with the Captain, but he had got to the stage where he couldn't really care less. Dud was used to getting the sack, and what did it matter what the Captain did or thought anyway?

This devil-may-care attitude gave the repulsive Dud bravado. He'd have one more go at impressing the boss, and if that didn't work – so what!

'Ah . . . Cheque,' said his boss, from behind his large desk.

'Yes Guv,' said Dud Cheque from in front of it.

'Today, Cheque,' said the Captain in a determined way, and looking Dud straight in the eye, 'you and I, buddy boy, are going to sort out, once and for all, how we get that blasted car of mine back. Get it?'

'Yes Chief,' said Dud Cheque.

'Yes,' the Captain went on. 'We've got to find some way of getting that ridiculous ton-up housewife to part with it. It's more than just the car, Cheque, it's . . .' he paused; there was no way that he could let the detestable Dud Cheque know about the Association of Bent Car Dealers, '. . . it's my honour that's at stake, my honour; understand?'

'Yes, Guv,' said Dud Cheque, though he hadn't a clue what the Captain was on about.

'Right,' said Captain Smoothy-Smythe. 'There is no device, trick or crime that we will not stoop to in order to get that Jag back. Right?'

'Right, Boss,' said Dud Cheque.

'Right, Cheque,' said the Captain and then he snarled, 'GET THINKING!'

'Right, Boss,' said Dud confidently, though he hadn't got the slightest idea what to think about.

While this interview was taking place at the ABCD Garage, Mrs Pratt had come downstairs and started her housework. She had put her red motor-bike racing leathers in the sink to soak. 'I shan't be needing those for a while,' she said to herself. 'I think my biking days are over. It's four wheels for me from now on, though I may still do a bit of two-wheel stuff on tight corners!' She chuckled with glee at the thought of it.

Wally put his cereal bowl on the draining-board.

'Right, Wallace!' she said to him. 'Today is a big day. We are going out in the Jag to get your cousin from the station. I'm going to put it through its paces!'

'Can Bean Pole, Bill Stickers and Ginger Tom come?'

'Yes. We'll leave in about an hour. Now out of my way, I've got to do the cleaning and the polishing.'

She picked up a tool-box full of cleaning things and went out through the front door. She spent the next hour polishing things under the bonnet of the Jaguar.

All this time the creepy and revolting Dudley Cheque had been thinking.

He had been doing his normal duties around the garage – he'd added paraffin to a new delivery of petrol, he'd helped Grimey O'Reilly to fill in the rust-holes in the wing of a Vauxhall Viva with newspaper and plaster before it could be painted over, and he'd wound back a couple of speedos, but his heart had not been in his work: he had been brooding.

He had been thinking of some way to impress the Captain, and to help him to get back his beloved Jaguar.

You may have realized that Dud Cheque is not a genius; he is a simple soul. Simple and dishonest.

'I know,' he said to himself suddenly, 'I'll keep tabs on the old girl! I'll tail her, follow her. If I follow her close enough I'm bound to get an opportunity to push her in a ditch, or nick the old car when she ain't looking. Simple!'

Having decided on this simple and dishonest course of action, Dud put it into operation straight away. He slipped out of the side door of the workshop and went round the back to a hut where he had put the motorbike he had taken in part-exchange from Wally's mother the day before. It roared into life, and a moment later Dud and the bike emerged from the hut like a bullet from a gun. He roared off in the direction of the recreation field, and if you'd seen him you would probably have guessed that he had never ridden a motorbike before in his life!

Bean Pole, Bill Stickers and Ginger Tom arrived together at Wally Pratt's front gate.

'Good morning Mrs Pratt,' they said to her, as she leant deep into the engine compartment of her massive new car. 'We like your car!'

'I should think you do!' said Mrs Pratt. 'It's got overhead cams, a high-compression engine and twin carbs. It should do nought to sixty in under eight seconds!'

'Can we all go out in it?' asked Bean Pole.

'Yes, I've just told Wally that you can; we're all going to the station in a tick to collect his little cousin April.'

Wally tore himself away from breakfast television and joined them at the front gate.

For the next half-hour or so while Mrs Pratt fiddled about under the bonnet of the car, the boys explored it, climbing in and out of the back. Mrs Pratt asked them to find the tool kit, which they eventually did – under a flap in the floor of the boot.

The car was nothing like any car the boys had been in before. Inside it smelt of leather and polished wood.

'Right!' said Wally's mum. 'Get in, you ghastly creatures, and hold on to your hats!'

They all got in, she pressed a button and the starter-motor whirred into action. In a trice, and a swirl of smoke and gravel, they were off!

This whole delightful scene had been witnessed, from behind a tree on the recreation ground opposite, by Mr Dudley Cheque.

9

A Problem for Dud Cheque

The Jaguar turned down in the direction of the ABCD Garage and Old Codger's Wood, and Dud Cheque, seeing which way it was heading, got the motorbike out from behind a bush where he had hidden it. After a bit of difficulty he got the engine started and set off in hot pursuit.

He roared down the hill towards the garage, his eyes fixed on the road ahead, anxious to catch a glimpse of the red car.

As he approached the garage he still couldn't see it, but he could see Captain Smoothy-Smythe. He was standing on the grass in front of the pumps and he was staring at Dud, his mouth open in disbelief. He also looked rather cross!

Dud pulled on the brakes, and came to a slithering halt beside his lord and master.

'Cheque! What the blazes . . .'

'Quick, Guv, jump on! I'm on to something!'

The Captain climbed on to the seat behind Dud, though he instantly regretted it.

The bike shot forward, doing wheelies down the road.

'CHEQUE! WHAT THE DICKENS DO YOU THINK YOU'RE DOING! FATHEAD!' shouted the Captain at the top of his voice.

'I'm following that Mrs Pratt and your car!' yelled Dud, above the roar of the engine.

Before the Captain could ask Dud Cheque what on earth he meant, a tractor pulled out from a farm gate. Dud swerved round in front of it, and then the bike went up a grass bank, through a hedge and across the corner of a small field before going through the hedge and back on the road again.

'ARE YOU TRYING TO KILL ME?!! DUNDERHEAD!' roared the Captain, turning quite pale. 'Have you ever driven one of these machines before?'

'No!' said Dud over his shoulder. 'Good, aren't I?'

'LET ME OFF!!'

'Course not!' yelled Dud. 'I'm following yer Jag – we'll see it soon, with a bit of luck!'

Meanwhile in the Jaguar, which was only a small distance ahead, everyone was having a very pleasant time. Mrs Pratt was very pleased with the way the car handled, and the boys sank back in the luxurious leather seats and let the world go by.

'It doesn't oversteer when you heel-and-toe!' said Wally's mother. 'And you don't need to double de-clutch – the synchromesh is still great!'

'What is your mother talking about?' whispered Ginger Tom to Wally.

'Search me!' said Wally.

'By the way, Wally,' said his mother, 'what is this Bags of Fun thing that April was on about on the phone? She says she may be on it this week, and will need a lift to London.'

'It's a TV show, Mum. Everyone watches it. If you didn't spend so much time in the kitchen mending motorbikes you'd know what it was!'

'Is your niece going on it, Mrs Pratt?' asked Bean Pole eagerly.

'Course she's not!' interrupted Wally. 'She's got no chance! Hundreds of people must write in asking.'

Moments later the car arrived at the small country railway station.

'Right, you lot! Stay there while I go and see if April's train has arrived yet,' said Mrs Pratt. She got out of the car and went into the station.

As she did so a motorbike came to a rather abrupt halt on the far side of the car park. Its front wheel went half-way through a length of wooden fencing.

'There they are, Guv!' said Dud, nodding towards the Jaguar.

'Just what in heaven's name do you think you are trying to achieve, Cheque?!' demanded the Captain, getting off the back of the bike.

'Well, Boss, I'm following the old girl . . . I reckon that if we spy on her we should get the chance to push her in a ditch or pond or summat, and nick your car back . . . I'm trying to impress you, Guv.'

'IMPRESS ME!' the colour was returning to the Captain's cheeks, in fact he was turning bright red. 'Impress me! If I hadn't got a sore foot from kicking large stones I'd impress it on the seat of your ghastly trousers! OAF! Of all the weak-headed, nincompoop schemes I've ever heard of, the idea of trailing round after this Mrs Pratt woman with a view to pushing her in a pond and nicking my car back is the most pathetic! If that's your idea of inventive crime you've got no place in a garage. Not *my* garage, at least!'

The Captain was furious!

Dud realized that he was about to get the sack, but he was saved for the moment by the fact that out of the corner of his eye he saw Mrs Pratt, a small girl and a grey dog coming out past the ticket collector.

'There she is now: get down behind this fence, Guv, quick!'

Captain Smoothy-Smythe and Dud Cheque got down behind the damaged fence.

'Right, you lot!' said Wally's mother when she got to the car. 'This is your cousin April Phoole, Wally, and this is her dog.' Then she indicated the other boys to April, and said, 'These are Wallace's little friends.'

'Hi there, you guys!' said April to the boys. She was small and round with fair hair and red cheeks. Wally Pratt didn't much like the look of her.

She got into the front of the car; so did her dog.

It was the scruffiest animal the boys had ever seen.

'I like your dog!' said Bill Stickers.

The dog obviously also liked Bill Stickers because it jumped over into the back of the car and started sniffing him.

'Cor!' said Bean Pole. 'It don't half look a mess. Where did you find it – in a tumble-drier? What's it called?'

'His name is Fog, because he is grey and thick,' said April, and then she changed the subject. 'What a simply blissful motor-car, Aunt Vera!' she said.

'It's blissful all right!' said her Aunt Vera, and she leaned forward and pressed the starter-button. Once more the engine fired into life, and with crunching wheels they swept out of the car park and headed for home.

'Come on, Guv! They're off again!' said Dud.

'I am not getting on that infernal machine again Cheque! It's a hazard to life and limb. Look how my slacks are all creased!'

'Well you'll have to walk then, mate, because I'm off!'

'Hang on!' said the Captain – his bruised foot hurt quite enough without him having to think about walking all the way home. 'I'll come, but take it easy. And the moment we get back you're coming into my office, buddy boy, for a really good talking to!'

The Captain got back on the bike and Dud restarted the mighty engine. With a jerk and a jolt they careered off down the station drive.

'STEADY, Cheque, you half-wit!' yelled Captain Smoothy-Smythe.

'I'm doing me best, Guv! It's kind of powerful, you know.'

Before very long they were going extremely fast, and Dud was very pleased when he saw that the back of the red Jaguar was visible ahead of them. He was still certain that given the right chance he might be able to snatch the car back from under Mrs Pratt's nose!

The boys in the car had gone rather quiet.

Wally's mother and April had a long conversation, but the boys didn't feel like joining in.

'What are you going to be when you grow up?' Vera Pratt had asked at one stage.

'A film star, of course,' said April.

'OH, a film star, eh. Have you never thought of becoming a mechanic?' asked her aunt.

'Your dog is making funny noises!' interrupted Ginger Tom.

'What!' said Mrs Pratt.

'The dog is making sort of gurgling noises,' explained Wally.

'Oh dear!' said April, looking over her shoulder at the dog. 'I think he wants to be sick.'

'KNICKER ELASTIC!!' shouted Wally's mother. 'It can't be sick in my car! Especially not on the leather seats!'

'But we're nearly home, Mum!' said Wally, for they were indeed just by the recreation field duck-pond.

'So what!' said his mother. She stamped on the brake pedal and the car screeched to a stop. 'Get it out on the grass! Quick!'

Wally acted quickly. He got the car door open and the dog jumped out on to the grass.

It was sick. Wally and the boys looked the other way.

It is a pity in some ways that they did not look behind them, through the car's rear window – if they had, they would have seen that Dud Cheque and Captain Smoothy-Smythe were approaching the back of the car on a motorbike at very high speed.

When Dud saw the Jaguar's brake lights come on suddenly, and saw it come to a halt, he put the bike's brakes on with all his might. Both he and the Captain shut their eyes, and expected the worst.

What actually happened was that the front wheel of the motorbike locked, and the machine did a somersault. This threw Dud Cheque and the Captain into the air.

However, when they came down they didn't go into the back of the lovely old Jaguar.

They went into the duck-pond.

10

Arresting Experiences for the Captain

While Captain Smoothy-Smythe and his stupid assistant were flying through the air above the town duck-pond, April Phoole's dog Fog got back into the car and her Aunt Vera drove them all home.

Dud Cheque and his boss landed together in the dirty green water, and they sat there for a moment or two collecting their thoughts. Then the motor-bike joined them.

'Cheque,' said the Captain when he had cleared some pond-weed from his throat, 'you are without doubt the most pig-headed, incompetent belly-bum-boil that I have ever come across!!!!'

'What do yer mean?' said Dud Cheque. 'You haven't hurt yourself, have yer?'

'THAT,' said the Captain, 'DOES IT!' He turned to where Dud Cheque was sitting in the muddy water, put his hands round Dud's dirty neck, and started to strangle him.

'Cor . . . lay off, Chief, you're hurtin' me froat!'

'Er . . . excuse me, Sir,' said a voice behind them.

The Captain let go of Dud's throat. They both looked up.

'Excuse me, Sir,' said the owner of the voice again. 'Does this happen to be your motor bicycle?' It was Ivor Truncheon, the local policeman.

'Er . . . well . . . yes, I suppose it is,' said Captain Smoothy-Smythe.

'And would you and this rather damp-looking gentleman be the two persons whom I have just observed flying through the air with the said motor bicycle?' inquired PC Truncheon politely.

'Well, yes,' spluttered the Captain, 'I suppose we are.'

'I see,' said the constable firmly. 'Prior to your flight, were you not proceeding in an easterly direction, to whit, from the vicinity of Old Codger's Wood, upon the Queen's highway on the said motor vehicle?'

'So what if we was!' said Dud Cheque defiantly.

'Well, Sir, I observe that neither of you was wearing a crash helmet, and you was thereby contravening the law. I must ask you both to get out of that pond and accompany me to the station. The local magistrate deals very firmly with young skinheads like you, so be warned!'

'SKINHEAD!' exclaimed Captain Smoothy-Smythe, standing up in the water. 'SKINHEAD! I'm no skinhead. I'm a respected member of society! I'm an officer and a gentleman!'

'So am I!' said Dud Cheque!

'No you're not, Cheque, you're a creepy little twit!' said the Captain.

'Come on, you two, before I have the handcuffs on you for obstructing the traffic and causing an affray in a public pond.'

And the officer escorted the two of them to the local police station.

* * *

Much later that day Captain Smoothy-Smythe and Dud Cheque were returned by police car to the ABCD Garage. The very thought of having cops around the place would have given the Captain the shivers, but he already had the shivers from the experience in the duck-pond.

'Right! Come into my office, Cheque,' he said when they were alone.

Dud shuffled dejectedly into the office.

'Now then!' said the Captain when they were either side of the large desk. 'You have proved yourself to be a complete and utter waste of space, time and money, Cheque! Your pathetic little scheme of spying on Mrs Blasted Pratt was a dead loss from the start, and all it got us was very nearly killed, soaked to the skin, and arrested by the local copper. Before I dismiss you from my garage for ever, have you anything to say for yourself?!'

'Well . . .' said Dud, 'I don't think it was such a bad idea. At least while I was behind that tree this morning I was able to watch her, and I might have come across a chance to knock her on the head! At least I saw her messing about with that old car of yours!'

This news had a strange effect on the Captain. It seemed to calm him down; his eyes opened wider, and his bullying voice fell away to a whisper. 'What do you mean – you saw her messing about with the car?'

'Well, she and them four boys was messing about in the boot, they was looking for something I reckon. The boys was in and out of the back seats too. That was before they drove to the station.'

These words filled Captain Smoothy-Smythe with deep, chest-thumping horror. Were his worst fears confirmed? Had Mrs Pratt discovered the ABCD gear and the loot in the boot? – even before he could work out plans to get the precious car and its guilty secrets back!

Although it was only mid afternoon, he sank down in his office chair and poured himself a very large gin.

'Damn and blast,' he said to himself (or words to that effect). But he wasn't shouting, in fact he mumbled the words under his breath.

Dud Cheque was rather surprised by the way the boss had quietened down. Dud seemed no longer to be under imminent threat of instant dismissal. He kept talking. 'And we was able to see her collect her niece from the station, like she said she would when we saw her yesterday,' he said.

Now the Captain did not really hear this last sentence, because he was not concentrating on what his idiotic assistant was saying: he was thinking of things like a visit from the police.

But then a very strange thing happened.

As Dud heard himself say the sentence it gener-
ated in his own head the only criminally brilliant
idea he had ever had.

'We could nick 'er instead,' he said.

The Captain heard this, but again without
concentrating on it. Impatiently he repeated,
'"Nick her instead"? What on earth are you on
about, Cheque, you blithering idiot! Nick Mrs
Pratt?'

'No, Chief – *nick 'er niece*,' replied Dud. 'Kidnap
'er, like – *kidnap the old girl's niece and tell 'er she
can't have the kid back until she gives you your car.*
Her niece has come to stay, Guv,' he added,
just in case the Captain still hadn't got the hang
of his brilliant idea. It's frustrating to have a
good idea when people don't appear to understand
it.

But the Captain seemed to be brightening.

'My word,' he said, quietly and slowly. 'My jolly
old word! You may be on to something! Look
here,' he said, and a smile began to change the line of
his thin moustache, 'look here, Cheque, I may have
been a bit hard on you in the past – I've been under a
lot of pressure you know, work and things like that
– yes . . . I see . . . *we kidnap the kid, and the car's the
ransom! What could be better!*'

The Captain was now actually smiling at his
humble employee!

'Cheque, old man,' he said. 'You've actually impressed me! Here, have a gin, old boy, a Jolly Old Gin!'

11

Bags of Fun!

While the wicked Captain and Dudley Cheque were plotting their villainous plans down at the ABCD Garage, Mrs Vera Pratt, April Phoole and Wallace Pratt were having cups of tea in Mrs Pratt's kitchen.

'Sorry there isn't much for tea, dear,' said Mrs Pratt. 'I've been very busy lately, what with worn sprockets on the bike, and one thing and another.'

'That's all right, Auntie,' said April, not really sure what her extraordinary aunt was talking about.

'By the way, April, there's a letter here for you. It came today.'

'Oh. Let me open it. I think I know what it is,' she said.

Wally watched as April opened an official-looking envelope with a typewritten address on it.

'Hurrah!' cried April Phoole. 'It's from the television company. I *am* going to be on Bags of Fun! I think this will be my lucky break into show business!'

As Wally had said to his mother, Bags of Fun was a very popular programme. It had recently rocketed

to the very top of the viewing charts. Captain Smoothy-Smythe chuckled at it over his early evening gin and tonic. Dud Cheque laughed out of the side of his mouth at it, and the O'Reilly brothers threw back their heads and roared with laughter at it, often spilling their Guinness in the process.

'How have you managed that, April?' asked Wally, rather amazed.

'Mummy sent my name in,' said April, still reading the letter. 'I have got to go to the London studios tomorrow as I warned you, Aunt Vera. You will be able to take me, won't you? It will be my lucky break!'

'Of course! In fact a good hard spell up the

motorway will do the car good – it may help to burn off carbon from the plugs! What time have we got to be there?'

'At mid-day.'

'No problem!' said Mrs Pratt. 'But I think we had better get some petrol now, so that we start with a full tank.'

She got the car keys, while April and Wally got in the car. April thought it best not to suggest that Fog went too.

They were half-way to the ABCD Garage when Mrs Pratt let out one of her shrieks: 'Knicker elastic!'

'What's up, Mum?'

'The fuel gauge! That's what's up! Look, it's nearly empty!'

'Can't you just buy some more?' asked April.

'Of course we can, April, but the point is that we've used nearly a whole tankful today! When I bought the car yesterday it was full. I shall have to investigate this tonight. Perhaps the twin carbs are set a bit rich.'

Mrs Pratt steered the magnificent car on to the ABCD forecourt, and stopped beside a petrol pump.

'I hope the two blokes who run this place don't give me any cheek. I told them to buzz off yester-day!' she explained to April.

The Captain saw the red Jag drive on to the

forecourt. It made his heart beat fast to see it so nearly back in his grasp, and yet so far from it!

Dud went out to the pump.

Mrs Pratt wound down her window. 'Fill it up, no messing!' she said.

'Yes Ma'am,' said Dud. The wheels on the petrol pump whirred round, and the air was filled with the smell of petrol mixed with paraffin.

Captain Smoothy-Smythe watched the refuelling operation through his grimy office window. He saw Dud lock the trigger on the filler nozzle and walk up again towards the driver . . .

'Goin' all right, is it?'

'Very well, thank you,' said Mrs Pratt. 'It's a good piece of engineering, and a lot safer than motorbikes. It's not too difficult to come a cropper on a bike.'

'You're telling me, lady!' said Dud. His clothes were still rather damp.

'And I like the car,' said April in the front seat, 'because when you are in it people look at you!'

'Oh ah,' said Dud. 'I expect you likes having people look at you, do yer?'

'Yes I do, and tomorrow lots of people will look at me, because I'm going to London to be on Bags of Fun – it's going to be my lucky break into show business!'

'Oh ah,' said Dud.

'Well . . . ?' asked the Captain, when the car had

gone and Dud had returned to the office, 'what did the old faggot say to you?'

'Nothing much, Guv, but I did get something from the horse's mouth, if yer knows what I mean.'

'I haven't the foggiest what you mean,' said the Captain. 'What do you mean?'

'They're going to London tomorrow. The little girl is going to be on Bags of Fun!'

'Is she indeed!' chuckled the Captain. 'Jolly old is she!'

And although there was nobody around, he and Dud began to plan, in whispers.

'Right!' said Mrs Pratt. 'You had better go to bed early, April, if you are going to do your best on Bags of Fun tomorrow.'

'Good-night, Aunt Vera.'

'Good-night.'

'Mum?'

'Yes Wally, what is it? Be quick, I've got a bit of work to do on the car tonight.'

'Could Bean Pole and Ginger and Bill Stickers come with us tomorrow?'

'Yes!' said his mother instantly. 'Go and phone them and tell them to be here at eight sharp. Then go to bed yourself.'

'Thanks, Mum!' said Wally Pratt.

He did as she suggested.

Vera Pratt took her tool-box out from under the

stairs, got a new socket set from a kitchen drawer, and went out into the late summer evening.

Before long the night air rang with the metallic sounds of her setting to work on the vintage car.

12

The Third Day

Good-morning. It is now the third day of this story; if you have got here in less time than that – slow down! You're getting ahead of us!

When Wally Pratt, Bean Pole, Bill Stickers, Ginger Tom, Captain Smoothy-Smythe, Dud Cheque, Vera Pratt, April Phoole, the O'Reilly Brothers, Fog the dog and everyone else woke up, it was raining.

April had not had a very good night's sleep. Strange bedrooms are often difficult to get to sleep in, and every time she started to drop off she had been woken again by an unfamiliar sound, like – for instance – the noise of Aunt Vera working on her car.

By eight o'clock in the morning, however, everyone was ready to start for London. April had put on a very pretty frock, and the four boys were as smart as it was possible to get them without making structural alterations.

Everyone agreed that it would be a good idea to

leave Fog behind, so they said good–bye to him and
then they all piled into the Jaguar. Mrs Pratt released
the handbrake and they were off.

In some ways the car was even more impressive
in the rain. Its paintwork had a glossy gleam, and
the tyres were black and shiny, like coal. The engine
was so quiet that the wet roads gave off a hissing
sound as the spray swirled behind them.

As they trundled along the motorway the sky
grew a little lighter, and the rain began to ease off.
The road started to dry in steaming patches and
small gaps of watery blue appeared between the
clouds.

Wally's mother was wearing a new white leather

flying helmet, which was fixed firmly under her chin, and chauffeur's white gauntlet gloves. She drove with a determined look on her face, and she gritted her teeth and put her foot down hard on the accelerator. From time to time her eyes strayed from the road ahead to the petrol gauge.

Not very far behind them Captain Smoothy-Smythe and his assistant Dud Cheque were also on their way to London. They were likewise trundling along the motorway, but on a rather tatty motorbike that looked as if it had just been dragged out of a pond.

The Captain was doing the driving, with Dud behind him.

'I feel a dashed sight safer at the front, old man!' he shouted.

'I feel a blooming lot more scared on the back!' replied Dud Cheque, again shouting, not just because of the engine noise, but also because they both had crash helmets on that covered their ears.

'Can you still see 'em, Guv?' Dud asked.

'Of course I can! But I don't want to get too close in case the silly old bat goes and sees us!'

'Well watch out she don't brake all of a sudden, however far ahead she is!'

'Oh, don't you worry about that, Cheque: I'm quite wet enough in this rain without taking a dip in any more ponds!'

★   ★   ★

Before long the red Jaguar crossed the Thames, and Wally's mother brought it to a halt outside the huge television studios. A man in a brown uniform stepped forward to greet them. His coat had gold braid on its sleeves, and bright gold buttons, and he had a cap like an admiral's.

'Morning, then,' he said, 'can I 'elp yah?'

'Yes,' said Mrs Pratt. 'My niece here is going to be on Bags of Fun, and she's been told to be here for mid-day.'

'This letter says I've got to meet Terry Household-Word,' added April to him.

'Righcherrare then, ducks,' said the man. 'Park yer lovely motor over there in that bay where it says "Artistes and VIPs", then come back 'ere an' I'll direct yer.'

They parked and all got out; Wally's mum had a quick look at the petrol gauge before switching the engine off, smiled to herself, and locked all the doors. Then they crossed back over the road and spoke to the doorman again.

'Right. You goes to the lift, see,' said the doorman, 'then you goes to floor fourteen. You'll meet old Terry there.'

'Thank you,' said Mrs Pratt.

'Not at all, duck,' said the man. 'Good luck, little 'un.'

April liked being wished good luck, though she

wasn't so pleased about being called 'little 'un'. She didn't feel it was very film-starry.

When they got inside the huge entrance hall they saw the lifts – three sets of shiny metal doors. April also saw the door to the ladies loo.

'I won't be a moment, Auntie,' she said, 'I just want to powder my nose.' And off she went.

'What the heck's she on about?' said Bean Pole.

'Search me,' said Wally.

'She's going to the lavatory,' said Mrs Pratt.

'Perhaps you should go too, while you've got the chance.'

The boys went off through the door marked 'Gents'.

Mrs Pratt stood in the foyer and waited. Before very long the four boys returned; but there was no sign of April.

'What can have happened to April?' said Mrs Pratt. 'I had better go into the lav and find her.'

Just as she started off towards the door, it opened and April emerged.

'Sorry about that, you guys,' she said. 'I had to fix my hair.'

'You gave me quite a scare,' said her aunt. 'I thought for a moment we'd lost you!'

They all got into one of the lifts and it zoomed up to floor fourteen, pressing their weight into their shoes as it did so.

Just as the doorman had said, they were met at the top by a group of people including Terry Household-Word and a tall girl who always appeared on Bags of Fun and was referred to as The Lovely Michelle.

The Lovely Michelle was dressed in a sparkling swimming costume.

A woman with a clip-board under her arm advanced from the group of people who were round Terry.

'Hi there,' she said directly to April, in an

American accent. 'You must be little April Phoole –
your momma wrote me about you! I'm Pamela and
I'll be looking after you from here on in.'

'Hello,' said April. 'This is my aunt, Mrs Vera
Pratt.'

'Well, hi there Vera!' said Pamela.

'Hi there,' said Mrs Pratt, and she took off her
white leather flying helmet and smiled. 'I have my
son and three of his friends here. They would like to
join me in the audience.'

'Well, that's just fine,' said Pamela, 'just fine.
I'm afraid Mr Household-Word is kinda busy
right now, so if you folks would like to make
your way through that door over there and take
the elevator to Studio 34A, I'll look after little old
April here and we'll meet you back here right after
the show!'

'Good luck, April!' said Mrs Pratt.

'Good luck,' said the boys.

Wally Pratt, his mother and his friends then went
through the double doors that Pamela had indicated. They got into another lift and made for
Studio 34A.

The whole building was like a rabbit warren.
Corridors went everywhere, and glass panels in the
doors revealed glimpses of rooms of every size.
There were obviously lots of offices, but every now
and then, as they struggled to find their way to
Studio 34A, they caught sight of large TV studios,

and went past red lights that flashed above notices that said SILENCE PLEASE RECORDING IN PROGRESS.

Eventually they found Studio 34A. A man in jeans and a tee-shirt was standing at the door, and several people were going through it.

'Is this the right place for Bags of Fun?' Mrs Pratt asked him.

'That's right,' he said. 'It'll start before too long, in you come.'

The studio was enormous. The stage and the seats for the audience only occupied a fraction of it. There were large expanses of darkness beyond the flimsy scenery.

The seats were raked very sharply so that people at the back were perched way up above the stage, which was on floor level. The seats at the front were almost on the stage, and there were cameras and wires everywhere.

They found some seats in the middle, next to one of the two aisles.

There was plenty to look at. The cameras were on hydraulic platforms, and the crews were busy testing them, moving them up and down. The stage looked just as it did every week on the television.

There were people everywhere. Men with earphones on moved around between the cameras, and others with clip-boards like Pamela's looked up at the lights and said things into small hand-held radios.

The lights dimmed.

'This is rather exciting, lads!' said Wally's mother. 'It reminds me of the feeling you get just before the start of a Grand Prix!'

The boys simply nodded. They were excited too.

Far below, outside in the street, two people and a rather tatty motorbike came to an abrupt halt when it accidentally hit the back of a parked police car.

13

April Phoole's Day

When the lights went dim the audience went quiet.

A voice over the sound system said, '*Ladies and gentlemen! Your compère and host for this edition of Bags of Fun! As always – Mr Terry Household-Word!*'

The lights lit up, even brighter than they had been before, and the ever-smiling Terry Household-Word stepped out of the darkness on to the back of the stage. Everyone clapped as he came to the front and spoke directly to the audience.

'Hello there, ladies and gentlemen. We haven't started recording yet but it's very good to be able to welcome you all to yet another edition of Bags of Fun. I hope you're all going to behave yourselves, mind!' The audience chuckled. 'As long as you just all sit there, and laugh when we tell you to, that'll be just fine! And no cuddling up there at the back!' He pointed to the seats way behind Mrs Pratt and the boys. 'This isn't a cinema, you know. You're not here to enjoy yourselves!'

Everyone laughed.

'All right for levels, George?' Terry asked a man near one of the camera crews. The man nodded and gave him a thumbs-up sign. Then the lights went down again, and the show began.

The rules of Bags of Fun were pretty simple. The game basically consisted of members of the public trying to guess the identities of a panel of famous celebrities who sat behind small illuminated desks with large paper-bags over their heads. The contestants could prod and poke the celebrities, but they couldn't take their paper-bags off.

The more famous people you guessed, the more prizes you won!

'OK! Rolling!' said a voice in the darkness.

The signature tune came out of loudspeakers, Terry came on again, everyone clapped and cheered, and the first two contestants were introduced to each other.

The first contestant was a man called Derek who got three personalities right and won a dining-room table and chairs. A girl called Monica then guessed David Bellamy and Jimmy Savile and won a night out in Birmingham, all expenses paid.

Then April came on. Under the lights she looked very small and rather pale. The Lovely Michelle brought her forward to be officially interviewed by Terry Household-Word.

'Now, who have we here, Michelle?' he asked. 'Here's someone who's going to win a few boys' hearts in days to come, eh!'

And the audience smiled.

'What's your name then, sweetheart?' said Terry,

bending down and putting the mike close to April's small face.

'I'm April,' said April.

'April, eh,' said Terry. 'Well you're looking very pretty today, aren't you, April?'

'Yes,' said April.

The audience laughed.

Then Terry went on to talk to April's opponent, who was a large teenager.

'Now then, and what's your name?'

'Andy,' said the young man. 'Andy Cuff.'

'Well, Andy, what are you going to be when you leave school?'

'A policeman,' said Andy.

'Oh, I see,' said Terry. 'So you'll be Andy Cuff with the 'andcuffs!'

How the audience roared!

Then the game got under way. Andy was to have first go. He advanced on the panel and started to try to identify them.

He took hold of one of the paper-bagged heads and poked and prodded it.

'I think I know this one, Terry,' he said eventually. 'I think it's Toyah Willcox!'

It was important of course that the other contestant could not know whether his opponent was right or wrong, so The Lovely Michelle now had the job of guiding the panel member into a special sound-proof box, referred to as the 'De-Bagging Box', where their identity would be revealed for all the viewers.

The person Andy Cuff reckoned was Toyah was led into the De-Bagging Box. It turned out to be Les Dawson, and everyone had a good laugh.

Now it was April's turn. She got Esther Rantzen straight away because she could feel her big front teeth through the paper-bag. Then she guessed Lenny Henry.

The audience applauded her wildly, especially because if you got three right in a row you had the chance of a Star Prize!

Next she got Ronnie Corbett: she knew it was him because he was smaller than she was.

If you were going for a Star Prize something special happened. You had to guess the identity of one more celebrity, but this time *your* head was in a paper-bag as well!

The Lovely Michelle and Terry Household-Word took April to have her own paper-bag fitted. This was done in a spectacular way.

What happened was this. April was put on a special Star Prize platform which was a round turn-table in the middle of the stage. It was about the size of a large round dining-table, and it rotated. It was divided in two by a tall upright division, so that you only saw the front half of it – a 'D' shape.

When a contestant had to be fitted with a paper-bag so that they could try for a Star Prize they stood on this front half of the turntable. The lights flashed,

the music played, and the platform slowly rotated so that the panellist disappeared from view.

When the turntable completed its revolution and the person appeared again, they were complete with a paper-bag on their head.

So The Lovely Michelle helped little April on to the front half of the Star Prize platform.

The audience were on the edges of their seats with delight and excitement! A child had never won a Star Prize before!

April stood on the platform, the lights went crazy, flashing in great arches above it, and an organ played loudly.

The turntable began to turn and April, wobbling slightly, disappeared backstage. The empty half of the platform came to the front, paused for a moment, and then started turning again, to complete its revolution.

When the original front half reappeared, April Phoole was not on it.

14

Call the Police!

'CUT!' shouted the man called George.

'WHAT IN HEAVEN'S NAME!' shouted Terry Household-Word, furiously.

'WHERE IS SHE?' called out lots of people.

Chaos broke out: the crews started shouting at one another, and most of the audience stood up to try and get a better view of what was going on. Where could their favourite contestant suddenly have got to!

Vera Pratt sprang to her feet: she clenched her large fists and strode down towards the stage. No TV company was going to lose her prize-winning niece.

The boys got up too, and before they knew what was happening they were trotting down the aisle towards the stage behind Wally's mum, like a small cavalry charge.

Terry Household-Word had rushed forward to speak to the man called George.

'WHERE THE HECK IS SHE?' Terry demanded.

'HOW DO I KNOW?' shouted back George, dropping his clip-board. 'REG!' he shouted, 'turn the Star Prize platform round again!'

Someone called Reg pressed a button and the platform began to rotate quite fast. There was still no sign of April.

'IDIOT!' shouted Terry Household-Word. 'Stop that blasted thing!'

'SHUT UP, FATTY!' called a voice in the darkness – presumably Reg's.

Terry Household-Word was just about to answer back when he tripped over a wire and fell headlong across the stage, which was already full of people rushing around.

Mrs Pratt and the boys arrived in the middle of the stage at the same time, and Wally, who took a bit more time to stop than the others, fell headlong over Terry Household-Word – the nation's most famous TV-show host.

'NOW WHAT . . . !' shouted Terry from the floor.

'CALL THE POLICE!!!' shouted Mrs Pratt. 'My niece has gone missing on television!'

Andy Cuff, who had been standing at the edge of the stage, realized that his chance had come!

'NO NEED TO CALL THE POLICE!' he shouted. '*I'M* HERE!'

When Wally tripped over Terry Household-Word it sent him into a head-first dive.

There was a tearing sound, and he went straight through the scenery at the back of the TV stage.

It was made of material far too flimsy to stop him. He landed in the dark on the other side of it, and he was quickly joined by Bean Pole, Bill Stickers and Ginger Tom, who had all been nimble enough to jump over Terry and nip through the large hole in the scenery made by Wally.

Bean Pole helped Wally up, and then all four of them looked round to see where they were.

What they saw, in the far distance, going through a door at the back of the studio, were two figures.

Although there was not a lot of light the boys could see that they were carrying a bundle between them that was undoubtedly April with her head in a paper-bag. One of the two had a shuffling, round-shouldered way of moving which they instantly recognized.

'IT'S THAT CREEP FROM THE GARAGE!' shouted Bill Stickers.

'Blimmin'eck – it is as well,' said Wally, rather out of breath.

'QUICK! POLICE! They're over here!' shouted the boys: as they did so the whole of the back of the stage crashed to the ground.

Out over it poured several of the people I've already mentioned. Andy Cuff led the charge, closely followed by Terry Household-Word, Wally's mother with raised fists, George and Pamela with their clip-boards, and several rather bewildered famous celebrities with bags on their heads who had very little idea what was happening.

'OVER THERE! THROUGH THAT DOOR! IT WAS THE MAN FROM THE GARAGE!' yelled Wally, and he and the boys joined in the pursuit.

Just as most of the pursuers got to the door at the very back of the huge studio, and when quite a few of them had got through it, the kidnappers of little April made a fundamental mistake.

They had rushed with her through the door at the back but, as you know, the TV company's head-quarters was like a rabbit warren. They turned down a corridor and went through the next door on the right.

The door brought them straight back into Studio
34A. They arrived back beside the famous De-
Bagging Box! Wally, Bean Pole, Bill and Ginger
were just leaving the studio when they heard the
kidnappers re-enter it: they swung round and saw
them.

'QUICK! OVER HERE!' they shouted, and the
four made a charge towards the criminals.

The scene now had all the classic ingredients of a
first-class scrum. Half the pursuers turned on their
heels, along with the boys, and the other half kept
going – down the corridor and towards the door
that would bring them all back into Studio 34A!

'It *is* those men from the garage!' shouted Bean Pole, as Captain Smoothy-Smythe and Dud Cheque, still holding April, advanced on them across the studio.

'GET THEM!' yelled Wally Pratt.

The Captain, Dud Cheque and the unfortunate April stopped and turned round, but Wally, Bean Pole, Bill Stickers and Ginger Tom kept going.

Wally Pratt was first-rate at bursts of instant action and, even if he lacked stamina, he could throw his weight into something for a short sharp moment.

Well, he threw his weight into Dud Cheque.

He brought him to the ground with a mighty wallop and a split second later Wally was sitting on Dud Cheque's head.

'GERRROFF!' said Dud Cheque, 'I never touched 'er!'

'NOW GET THE BLOKE IN THE BLAZER!' yelled Wally.

Bean Pole, Bill Stickers and Ginger Tom did as they were told: they dived at the Captain's check trousers in a rugger tackle that could have put all of them into the England team.

As Bean Pole, Bill Stickers, Ginger Tom, the Captain and April all joined Wally and Dud Cheque on the floor, the scrum that I predicted happened.

Half the pursuers, including Wally's mother and George and Pamela and Terry Household-Word and Reg, who had kept on going down the corridor and through the door, collided with members of the Bags of Fun audience and panel who had turned on their heels in the studio.

Andy Cuff was one of the first on the scene.

He knew that if he could make an arrest now his career in the police force would get off to a good start. He had gone round the corridor route to the scene of the scrum, and on the way he had done a very intelligent thing.

He had picked up from a small table beside the frantically spinning Star Prize platform a spare paper-bag. Knowing that he had no handcuffs, he had an instinctive, law-officer's feeling that a stout paper-bag could serve an excellent purpose if someone had to be arrested rather sharply.

At the very moment when he arrived at the general tumble and scrummage of bodies, he heard Wally shout: 'GET THE BLOKE IN THE BLAZER!'

It was Andy Cuff's bad luck that Terry Household-Word happened to be wearing a very nice blue blazer.

In an instant Andy had the large paper-bag over the famous man's head.

'IRISH-STEW-IN-THE-NAME-OF-THE-LAW!' he shouted, breathlessly. 'Youarenotobliged!' he panted, 'tosayanythingbut! Anythingyoudosay maybetakendown . . .'

'GET OFF! You daft twit!' shouted Terry Household-Word.

'Andusedinevidenceagainstyou – so – help – me – god!' continued the teenage policeman in one breath.

People fell over other people. Terry Household-Word, paper-bagged, aimed a punch in the general direction of Andy Cuff who was looking around for a notebook, but it hit the man called George. George mistakenly hit Reg on the head with his clip-board, and so did Pamela – she had never liked Reg.

Mrs Pratt still called for more highly trained police assistance: 'THEY HAVE GOT MY NIECE!' she shrilled. 'CALL THE POLICE!'

'I'M ALREADY HERE!' yelled Andy Cuff, and then Reg knocked him out with a blow on the jaw.

At about this time the De-Bagging Box exploded.

It was probably caused by people disturbing the wires that led to it. A high-tension wire inside it must have touched a bare nail-head or something and WUMPHHHHF! There was a huge flash, and most of the studio lights went out.

The general shock of the explosion stopped people in their tracks. They got up very quickly, and dusted themselves down. Those who weren't really very involved in trying to find poor April or catch the criminals realized that they'd been carried along too far in the general excitement of the chase.

Wally stood up, and looked in the semi-darkness

for Bean Pole, Bill and Ginger. He had Dud Cheque by his greasy collar. 'This is one of them!' said Wally.

'No I ain't,' said Dud, 'I dunnow anythink about it!'

'So where is April?' asked Mrs Pratt, expecting to find her among the large pile of people who were recovering on the studio floor.

Wally looked, and Bean Pole looked, so did Bill Stickers and Ginger Tom. She was not there: neither was Captain Smoothy-Smythe.

'QUICK!' said Mrs Pratt. 'He's got away! Quick boys, *QUICK!*'

Wally released Dud Cheque and joined his mother and the boys as they raced for the studio door. They all knew instinctively that the only way to get April back now was to get to the main door before the cunning Captain got away.

Dud Cheque stood up and surveyed the general confusion. Terry Household-Word was taking a paper-bag off his head, and an ambulance was being called for Andy Cuff. Reg was saying something very rude to Pamela, and George was putting out the fire in the De-Bagging Box.

'That kid must weigh 'arf a ton,' Dud said, rubbing his head.

Then he shuffled off, round-shouldered, into the shadows and out of this story.

15

Curtains for Captain Smoothy-Smythe

Vera, Wally, Bean Pole, Bill Stickers and Ginger Tom were right in their assumption that the only way to get April back was to try to intercept the Captain at the front of the studios.

At that very moment the Captain was running down the main stairs with her under his arm. What's more, he happened to have in his pocket the spare keys for the Jaguar, from the board in the ABCD Garage workshops.

As he raced downstairs as fast as his suede shoes would carry him, Mrs Pratt and the boys raced downstairs as fast as the lift would carry them.

The Captain got there first.

April Phoole had almost given up struggling. Although she was quite a spirited girl in her own way, she had had a lot to put up with. She had faced meeting one of the country's top celebrities, and had appeared before the TV cameras of the nation. She had very nearly won a Star Prize and she'd been involved in a fight with a lot of very rough adults. Now she was being kidnapped. It had not been her day, after all.

'Er . . . excuse me, my good man,' said Captain Smoothy-Smythe breathlessly when he finally arrived in the foyer.

'Yes mate?' said the doorman in the brown uniform.

'This poor little girl's been taken ill. I believe she arrived here in an old Jaguar – can you tell me where it's parked?'

'Sure fing, mate,' said the doorman. 'There it is – over there, in the bay marked for artistes and VIPs.'

'Thanks very much,' said the Captain, and hitching April a little higher under his arm he set off across the road.

As he did so he felt very pleased with himself. The inventive kidnap scheme that he and Dud Cheque had devised had gone wrong, but now he'd got the kid, and there was the precious car too – with its loot in the boot. He'd got more than he'd ever hoped for: with so many trump cards up his sleeve how could he fail now?

As the Captain set off across the road towards the car, the lift doors slid open and out came his pursuers. Seeing no sign of him or April in the entrance hall they went through the glass doors at the front of the building, and out on to the front steps.

It didn't take them very long to see what needed to be done next. Over the road stood the Captain. He was shutting the back door of the Jaguar.

'Quick, Wally,' said Ginger Tom. 'There he is!'

'Come on!' said Wally – an unusual expression for him.

'Let's go, daddy-oh!' yelled Vera Pratt, rolling up her sleeves.

They started off across the street. Although the boys, led by the nippy Ginger Tom, began in front, Wally's mother showed amazing speed.

By the time they reached the cat's-eyes in the middle of the road they were neck and neck, again like a small cavalry charge.

The Captain had a key in the lock of the driver's door and one hand on the door handle when Mrs Pratt got up to him.

If, at that moment, she had tried to scratch his eyes out, or pull his hair, or beat in rage on his chest, he would no doubt have thrown her to the ground and driven off.

Luckily Vera Pratt was made of sterner and less conventional stuff. As she got to him she slowed down, hitched up her skirt, and pulled from the top of her stocking a huge adjustable spanner.

The Captain's mouth dropped open in amazement, but it closed again very quickly when she swung the spanner back like a sword, brought it up sharply, and caught him under the chin with it.

There was a gravelly sound of crunching teeth, and a WHOOSH of suddenly expelled air as Captain Smoothy-Smythe – villain and deceiver – fell to the ground. As he slithered to earth his moustache slipped to one side, and then fell on to his chest. It was obviously as false as he was.

The boys were astounded.

'Cor . . . Mum! . . .' began Wally.

'Never mind "Cor Mum". Where's April?' said his mother.

'Search me,' said Wally.

There was no sign of her anywhere.

'There's only one thing to do,' said Mrs Pratt, woman of action. 'Put him in the car and we'll head for the nearest police station!'

'Right,' said Bean Pole. 'Come on, Wally, help me get him in the front.'

The four boys and Mrs Pratt got the front door of the car open, and lugged the groaning figure of Captain Smoothy-Smythe on to the front seat.

A purple tie was lying on the floor at the back of the car.

'Hey, I didn't notice this before,' said Bill Stickers, 'but we might as well tie his feet together with it.'

'Let me,' said Bean Pole. 'I'm good at knots.'

'Right!' said Mrs Pratt as she got the car going, 'hold on to your hats!'

But they had only gone a very short way when they heard a groaning sound.

'Hey,' said Bill Stickers, 'there's something up with this back seat – it's all lumpy.'

'And it's making noises,' said Bean Pole.

'Stop the car, Mum! I reckon we've found her!' shouted Wally.

Wally's mum stopped the car, and as it stopped the back seat seemed to erupt like a small volcano. The boys fell forwards off it and it tilted up at the front. They peered under it and saw April.

She was trussed up with several purple ties like the one they had just used to tie the Captain's feet together. One was serving as a fairly effective gag.

She was lying in a large cavity beneath the seat, which obviously contained several other things. It looked like the inside of a very large dressing-up box.

'Here she is!' shouted Wally excitedly.

'Get her out and see if she's all right!' said his mother.

'Are you all right?' Wally asked April, but she only replied with a look, because of the gag.

In no time they had her out and untrussed. She was obviously badly shaken, but when they managed to get the gag off her mouth she did have something to say.

'This has been the most disastrous day of my life!' she said. 'If this is showbiz, you can keep it! I'm through, *through*, I tell you! I quit! *Quit* – do you hear me! I never want to go near show business or the stage again! I've been a fool, a blind little fool! How was I ever taken in by the tinsel and the glitter! I'm going to do something good and sensible from here on in – in fact I'm going to take up horse-riding! I'm going to be one of the best jump jockeys the world has ever known! All I need is a lucky break! Just you see!' and she slumped down exhausted on the floor of the car.

While she was giving this speech, Wally Pratt had been reading.

He had been reading from one of many small books that he had come across as he was helping April from her prison under the back seat. The book was entitled, 'Association of Bent Car Dealers, Rule Book for Members'.

Then suddenly, from the road behind the car,

they heard the wailing whine of a police siren. A large white Rover, with red stripes and blue flashing lights, sped past them and then slammed on its brakes. It was packed with policemen.

'Good!' said Mrs Pratt. 'The police have arrived – now we can get this ghastly man arrested for nicking my niece!'

But the police car had actually stopped a little way ahead of the Jaguar. Policemen were pouring out of it, and clustering round a rather tatty old motorbike that was lying on its side in the road. Mrs Pratt and the boys then noticed that just ahead of the smashed bike was a second police car, with a bad dent in the back of it.

One of the policemen started to pull what looked like bits of pond-weed from round the engine of the bike, while others took out notebooks or started talking into their radios.

The sound of the police siren had an instant effect on the dazed brain of Captain Smoothy-Smythe. It was, after all, the sound he dreaded most in life. 'Where the devil . . .' he stammered.

'Watch out, boys, he's coming round!' warned Mrs Pratt.

'Where the devil . . . am . . . I? Where . . . the . . . devil . . . is my blasted moustache?' groaned the Captain. He felt as if he'd been kicked by a donkey.

'HEY . . . LISTEN TO THIS,' said Wally, and

he started reading from the small book. '"*Rule Five; all members must at all times wear moustaches, thin and black in colour. Members with insufficient or non-standard moustaches of their own must wear Mr Spiv's Special Stick-Ons, as given out on enrolment.*"'

'What on earth's going on?' said the Captain, now more wide awake. 'What do those cops want?' He had panic in his voice.

'AND LISTEN TO THIS!' said Wally, '"*The following members have the following vehicles without any registration documents . . . For sale, special price to members, genuine new tyres, all fell off the back of a lorry . . . Wanted . . . faked MOT certificates*' . . . *How to beat the Tax Man! . . . Caring for your false moustache!*"'. This is something to do with a criminal organization!' exclaimed Wally.

'It seems very interesting that our gallant Captain here now has no moustache!' said Mrs Pratt sarcastically.

'Now hang on, old girl, I can see what you're thinking,' said the Captain, preparing to talk his way out of the situation with his usual flattering tricks.

He didn't get very far.

'Look, sunshine!' she said. 'Just remember that police car over there! And this spanner.' She raised the adjustable spanner a few inches above the Captain's ruffled hair. 'My Wally and his mates have discovered your wicked Association, and you have been caught red-handed trying to kidnap my niece. I think it is you who should hang on!'

'Yes,' said Wally from the back seat. 'You can't go telling us to buzz off now, mister – you've had it.'

Captain Smoothy-Smythe saw that he was in trouble. The police were still examining the remains of the motorbike, not very far away, and that made him feel particularly jumpy. He also felt extremely uncomfortable without his moustache: it was rather like having to argue with someone when you have no trousers on. He felt naked without his Mr Spiv's Special Stick-On firmly in place.

Given more time, and less pressure in the form of the adjustable spanner, he might have attempted to talk his way out of the situation, but he knew he was in a very tight corner.

The Captain decided to bring our story to a close. He pulled out his fat wallet.

'OK, Madam,' he said, in a dignified way, 'I can see that you've got me up a creek without a paddle – as we used to say in the navy. I tell you what I'll do. You bought this old car for a thousand pounds' – and here the Captain tried to smile, despite the pain in his jaw. 'I admit that I may have seemed a bit of a bounder to you – but we won't go into all that now. I'll buy the old wreck back off you for . . . let me see . . . four thousand pounds!'

The boys were amazed. The Captain started to

count out the money, in fifty- and hundred-pound notes.

'Make it five,' said Mrs Pratt.

'Er . . . very well, Madam – I must say you drive a very hard bargain.'

'Yes, I do,' replied Mrs Pratt. 'And count it out slowly. I want to see every note.'

'I say,' said the Captain, 'don't you jolly well trust me?'

'No, I jolly well don't.'

The Captain finished counting out the five thousand pounds. Beads of perspiration stood out on his brow – he never liked parting with money, and he'd never before had to pay out cash to get his own car back, especially not at a loss!

His consolation was that he would be getting his hands on the safe full of money in the boot. The precious records of all the members' names and addresses would be his again: the splendid Association would manage to carry on and he wouldn't be hounded out of the motor trade. The more he thought about it, the better he felt.

'Oh well,' he said, in a relieved voice. 'As I said last time we met, I'm sure this car was not modern enough for you, my dear, and I expect you found it expensive to run. It certainly doesn't do many miles to the gallon!'

'Oh, it's not so bad,' replied Mrs Pratt, smiling sweetly to him as she and April and the boys got out of the car. 'It wasn't too good at first, but then I discovered a heavy old safe bolted in the boot. I had quite a job, but I managed to take it out last night and get it into my kitchen. You will find the miles per gallon much better now! Good-bye, Captain!'

And she and her niece and the boys walked off to find a railway station.

The Captain sat in his beloved Jaguar and stared blankly out through the windscreen.

Whether he saw the error of his ways, and re-pented, I cannot say, but somehow I doubt it.

Whether the resourceful Vera Pratt ever found a way to open that safe is something I don't know either, but I do know that later that year she put quite a large sum of money into the Post Office, and also bought a very impressive, brand-new motor-bike.

COME BACK SOON
Judy Gardiner

Val is disturbed when her scatty mother walks out and leaves her family. She soon learns much about herself and her relationships.

IN A CLASS OF THEIR OWN
ed. Barbara Ireson

A marvellous medley of twelve stories from talented and well known writers such as Jan Mark, Bernard Ashley, Antonia Forest, Iris Murdoch, Gene Kemp and Isaac Asimov. And all the stories are about school . . .

JASON BODGER AND THE PRIORY GHOST
Gene Kemp

A ghost story, both funny and exciting, about Jason, the bane of every teacher's life, who is pursued by the ghost of a little nun from the twelfth century.

SADDLEBOTTOM
Dick King-Smith

The hilarious adventures of a Wessex Saddleback pig, whose white saddle is in the wrong place, to the chagrin of his mother.

FRYING AS USUAL
Joan Lingard

When Mr Francetti broke his leg it looked as if his fish restaurant would have to close so Toni, Rosita and Paula decide to keep things going.

COME SING, JIMMY JO
Katherine Paterson

An absorbing story about eleven-year-old James's rise to stardom and the problems of coping with fame.